DEAD GROUND

ROD HUMPHRIS

Don 1/20.

a Simon Ellice story

First published in Great Britain in 2019 by Rat's Tales

Rat's Tales Publishing 6-7 Queen Street Bath, BA1 1HE

Copyright © Rod Humphris, 2019

The moral right of Rod Humphris to be identified as
the Author of this work has been asserted.

10 9 8 7 6 5 4 3 2 1

Book design by RantArt.
Illustration Copyright © Laura R. Molnar & Rat's Tales.

Printed and bound in Great Britain by T J International

A CIP catalogue record for this book is available
from the British Library.

ISBN: 9781999651701

The paper this book is printed on is certified by the © 1996
Forest Stewardship Council A.C. (FSC). It is ancient-forest
friendly. The printer holds FSC chain of custody SGS-COC-2061.

DEAD GROUND

To those who really know what this was like,

from one who can only guess,

respectfully.

The world was going on and I couldn't stop it. I didn't want to feel anything except my anger.

I left my pack at the door and went into the busy, low-ceilinged ops room of the patrol base Azun. Major James Snowhall was at his usual place in conference with Dan Granger, the 2IC. I stood to attention in front of them and said, "Sir."

"You're back, are you?" Snowhall said, looking up from his laptop.

"Yes, sir."

"I see. Well, you'd better get to work then."

"Yes, sir."

I hadn't expected much of a welcome. I turned and went towards the exit.

"Wait."

I stopped and turned round.

"Your men will be glad to see you. Gerald will get you up to speed. Come and find me at nineteen thirty."

"Sir."

I went out into the hard light. The mountains hanging over us had a dusting of snow and I knew that it would be cold later. I heft my pack onto one shoulder and walked the long way through the dust to the bases' living area. This took me past the mortar enclosure, the Javelin station and the main sangar from where we kept watch.

The sangar was a crude structure of timber, corrugated iron and sandbags perched on the Hesco wall at one side and on rough timber stilts at the other. The Hesco wall itself just a construction of massive gravel filled bags. It was all temporary and makeshift.

There were a group of men in full kit on QRF duty lounging about at the foot of the ladder. They called rough greetings to me which I returned with their name, or nickname. The tension seemed to have etched itself a little deeper into their faces. Mostly they turned back to their card games or play-stations, but some followed me with their eyes as I went on.

At the fifty cal I stood with Milton and Deaks for a few minutes and looked at the terrain. It hadn't got any better. There were children playing tag in the dust in front of the mosque and women moving about carrying their burdens.

"You're back then, Lieutenant Ellice, sir," Deaks said, giving me an exaggeratedly proper salute undercover of the wall.

"Yes, Deaks, I'm still a lieutenant. They haven't promoted me yet," I said.

That made them laugh.

"Good to have you back, sir," Milton said.

"Good to be back," I said.

"Really, sir?" Deaks said.

"Actually, yes, Deaks," I said.

"Fucking hell, sir," he said.

"Quite," I said.

I left them to it and went to look for Gerald. I found him in the tent that served us both as home.

"Fuck me. You're back," he said.

"Apparently," I said, pushing a pile of papers off an empty missile crate that was doing duty as a chair and sitting down.

"Does the OC know?"

"Just seen him."

"Oh."

"He's going to talk to me later. You're to fill me in."

"Okay. How did…? I mean, I didn't expect you back so soon."

"It was a funeral. They don't take long."

"Si, I didn't say…"

"Let's just talk about work, shall we."

"Oh, sure. Well, it's been fairly quiet. Just a little badly aimed sniping. Nothing nasty underfoot, thank God."

"Still no materiel, no Terry?"

"Nope."

"Glad I haven't missed anything. What about the ANAs?"

"Ah well, that's another story. They've managed to sell about half our fuel and Dan is beside himself about how they got it out without us knowing. One of them has been medevaced out. Shot in the leg by one of his mates. Your special friend has been his usual self. Again, all normal."

"And the noble endeavour?"

"Don't be sarcastic. No, they still aren't telling us shit. Omar Wardak could be having lunch with the jast right now for all we would know about it. The price of goats keeps on going up though. Never mind hearts and minds, it's fucking dollars and afs round here."

"How's the old man?"

"Stressed as fuck."

"Thought so. The waiting."

"It's not just that."

"No, I don't suppose it is. Are you training the ANAs now? This morning, I mean."

"In a minute, actually. You're not thinking of joining us?"

"No point putting it off. I'll take this afternoon's bimble too if you want."

"God, yes. If you don't mind."

"You do look a bit knackered."

"I'm trying not to think about it."

"Probably the best plan. I'll get coffee and meet you there."

"Okay, why not. What could possibly go wrong."

I got my personal weapon from the armoury and coffee from the canteen. Coffee would be an overstatement but it was warm and wet. On what passed for our parade ground Sergeant Nigel Hallatrow was looking pissed off and trying to hide it.

Hesketh and Thompson were with him, looking calm and professional, as usual. Hesketh, smiled at me and said, "Heard you were back, sir."

"Missed me, Hesketh?" I said.

"Not the same without you, sir," she said, looking at me closely, but pretending not to."

"Morning, sir. Good to see you back, sir." Hallatrow said. Now he looked worried as well.

"Thanks, sarg. Don't worry, I'll be good."

"Thank you, sir," he smiled, grimly.

"This it?"

Barely twenty of the forty or more Afghan National Army soldiers who were stationed with us had turned up for gravel bashing. They stood about looking bored. One of them had rested the muzzle of his M16 in the dirt and was leaning on the butt.

"Thompson, take the terp and see what you can do," Hallatrow said.

"Yes, sarg," he said, giving me a grin.

Thompson, not yet in his twenties but already looking older, went with Jadoon the interpreter to the tents pitched on the south side of the compound. His SA80 went with him and it wasn't just because we were all anticipating an attack.

"Bet you he doesn't come," Gerald said, joining us.

"I'm past caring," I said, handing him his coffee.

"God, I hope so," he said.

"You can go and get some rest if you want. I can do this."

"You won't do anything silly if I go?"

"Would it stop me if you're here?"

"It never has yet. Fuck, I'm tired."

"Go and lie down, you idiot."

"Okay, but I'll come running if anyone starts screaming."

He went, absentmindedly trying not to spill his coffee, and Thompson and Jadoon came back with half a dozen men straggling behind them. Lieutenant Emal Mirwais wasn't among them.

"Lieutenant Merwas says that he's brave enough and doesn't need to practice," Thompson said, with a perfectly straight face.

"Very good Thompson," Hallatrow said, with a barely perceptible sideways glance in my direction.

"Are you going to fetch him again, sir?" Thompson said, looking at me hopefully.

"No, I am not, Thompson," I said. "Carry on, sarg."

"PARADE. PARADE SHUN."

Hallatrow started doing his best to get the ANAs to stand up straight and form lines. Thompson helped him; pushing and shoving here and there. Hesketh and I just stood stolidly to one side; our personal weapons slung. It wasn't that we didn't trust them, it was just that we didn't trust them unless we could see them and they weren't armed.

Hallatrow, assisted by Thompson, did his best to get them to perform some semblance of parade drill, while Hesketh and I stood and watched and didn't show our feelings. The Afghanis didn't see the point, and by now, neither did we, but orders are orders. Hallatrow bore the brunt of it and we suffered with him. He got some poor kind of order and tried yet again to instil cohesion, discipline and teamwork, but it was a sham.

Just before I thought the first ANA would actually walk off I said, "Good job, sergeant. Shall we move on to small arms practice now?"

"Very good, sir," he said. "STAND AT EASE."

Jadoon repeated that in Pashto and Dari and the men stopped looking in our direction and started talking to each other.

I led the way to the improvised firing range and Hesketh and I had a little competition while the ANAs were collecting magazines for their M16s from the armoury. She beat me, as usual.

When the Afghanis were assembled I put a $50 note under the webbing on my helmet. Hallatrow, Hesketh and I took a man each while Thompson and the terp kept score. The task was to put three controlled bursts of four into the target with as tight a group as possible. The problem, as usual, was to get them to do more than just empty the magazine in the general direction of the targets and hope for the best.

I grabbed the barrel of the M16 that my ANA was about to swing across me and pointed it back towards the target.

"Inshallah," he said, shrugging, closing one eye and squeezing the trigger.

In a momentary pause in the firing I heard Thompson say, "Sir," and turned to see what was up.

Mirwais had deigned to grace us with his presence. He looked at the fifty on my helmet and held out his hand to the Pashtun nearest him for his M16. He said something in Pashto and Jadoon said, "Lieutenant Mirwais says, 'I shoot the best.'"

Everyone looked at me. I looked at Mirwais and, yet again, refrained from beating him senseless with the butt of a rifle. Instead I gestured towards the nearest firing station and gave him a sweet and ironic smile.

He looked at me suspiciously and then turned and emptied the magazine at the target. It wasn't completely bad shooting. I don't know if it was the best so far, but it may have been. He passed the gun back and stood there, waiting for me to give him the 50.

I looked at Hallatrow and he looked at me. It was all crap but it was what we had. We made a few more take their turn for the sake of it, but they weren't going to shoot better than Mirwais, even if they could. I called a halt to it and gave the order for the magazines to be collected up and returned to the armoury.

Mirwais stood in front of me and said something in Pashto. "Lieutenant Merwas says that he is waiting for his prize," Jadoon said.

Everyone stopped what they were doing to see what would happen. I let the rage in me build up until I was just slightly shaking with it and then slowly took my helmet off, extracted the note and held it out. Mirwais stepped forward, took it out of my hand and walked off.

The ANAs were talking and laughing as they went off towards the canteen tent. I took a deep breath said, "Good work, everyone."

"Why did you let him do that, sir?" Thompson said.

"It's important to maintain good working relations with our allies, Thompson," I said.

"But, sir, they're only…"

I gave him a look that stopped him in his tracks.

"… good working relations. Yes, sir."

"Who's on patrol with me this afternoon?" I said.

"Are you leading the bimble, sir?" Hesketh said.

"Yes, Hesketh. That alright with you?"

"Yes, sir. C section. All the old gang, sir."

"Good. Well, make sure you're fed, watered and rested. Okay?"

"Yes, sir," they said.

I went to wake up Gerald for some food.

Lunch was goat stew. Just for a change. Gerald didn't speak to me much and I didn't blame him. The rage was white-hot inside me and I expect it showed on my face. The atmosphere in the tent was subdued. Even Dobbs was quiet and that normally only happens when he's asleep.

Corporal Wykham came in, saw me and Gerald and came to our table.

"Briefing at fourteen hundred, sir?" he said, looking from one to the other of us.

"He's got it," Gerald said, nodding towards me.

"Briefing at fourteen hundred, sir."

"Thanks, corp," I said.

"Old man'll want you to go over the hill again," Gerald said.

"For whatever point there is in that," I said.

"I don't know if I'm more relieved you're back or more worried."

"Don't worry. What could possibly go wrong around here?"

At two o'clock I presented myself in full battle rattle in the ops room. The OC looked at me seriously and said, "Ah, it's you, Ellice. Good, I've got a job for you."

"You want me to go over the pass, sir."

"I simply don't believe nothing is coming in."

"I'd be happy to do a night shift, sir," I said.

"We've had that discussion, Ellice."

"Yes, sir."

"Just leave a team to keep watch while you do your social work."

"Any ANAs, sir?"

"On the hill? Best not. Keep them with you in the village. Any questions?"

"No, sir."

"Go and brief your men then."

"Yes, sir."

I walked to the canteen tent which was now serving duty as a briefing room for the patrol. There were sixteen riflemen, including C section, sitting on one side of the room and ten ANAs, including Mirwais on the other. Two interpreters, Jadoon and Wur were sitting at the front, one on each side. The ANAs were lounging about looking indolent and insolent as usual.

"ATTENSHUN," sergeant Waits said.

"At ease, gentlemen," I said, walking to the map pegged to a rope between two of the tent poles. "Now, listen up. This is the plan for this afternoon's little stroll…"

I pointed and set specific tasks to teams and waited while the interpreter Wur translated for the ANAs where necessary. A lot of it was the same old thing and I was only really saying it for the benefit of the ANAs. Like I cared.

"Right. You have your list of celebrities?" I said.

The men held up laminated cards with mug shots of known insurgent leaders. The narrow, mad-eyed face of Omar Wardak, warlord and king of the mountains top of the pile.

"Good. Let's go."

We filed out, crossed the short distance to the exit and rifleman Stains, who was on stag there, moved the wire barrier to let us out. As we stepped past the Hesco barriers the men at the main sangar would be scanning the village and the surrounding hills with extra care for the tell-tale muzzle-flash of enemy action.

We took the path that led over the slight shoulder of the rise on which the base stood and then down to the river. We were now in dead ground; the terrain that, because of the position of the base and the lie of the land, couldn't be viewed with line of sight by humans or the long-range sensors.

This path had been checked for IEDs first thing and had then been under direct observation by the team at the bridge since, so we stepped out without much fear of being turned into red mist.

Corporal Sykes, team leader at the bridge, nodded to me instead of saluting. The three Rifles with him acknowledged my arrival and then turned back to watching the paths. The four ANAs with them carried on lounging about looking bored. There were three small boys sitting on the bridge. They were tossing pebbles at the trout that hung in the streaming, turquoise water and waiting for something interesting to happen.

"Well, corporal?" I said.

"A few goats and a cow, sir," he said, smiling.

"No RPGs or KBMs?"

"Not that we've noticed, sir."

"What a surprise."

"Yes, sir."

"Carry on, corp. We're just off for a bimble."

"Nice day for it, sir."

We spread out to cross the narrow plank bridge, both so that it wouldn't sag too much and not to present too tempting a target for a watching enemy, and then turned left onto the main path. Behind us it wound down beside the river towards Paprock and before us it led to the village and then past it to the pass and beyond that to the next valley. We walked carefully upwards, looking for any signs of disturbed earth, but mostly the path was too rocky for anything to be buried.

When we got to the mosque Corporal Wykham looked at me. I nodded and he and his team of six stepped carefully down the bank into the main irrigation trench that fed the small, enclosed fields below and started following it. It would be a long, hard walk for them, made harder by the fact that for most of it they wouldn't use any of the paths. They would skirt the fields and then cut up to the pass.

I led the rest of us up the sloping rock and shale path into the village. It was hot walking in full kit and body armour under the strong sun.

The mountains of north eastern Afghanistan aren't an easy place to live, and they aren't an easy place to build houses either, but the Nuristani do it in some style. They stack them in tiers on the hillsides so that the roof of one is the patio of the one above. A village looks like one organic thing, not some buildings that happen to be near each other.

Several men of the village were waiting for us by the arched doorway into the first courtyard. Their faces were inscrutable but I was certain that they weren't happy. The ANAs, on the other hand had come out of their usual lethargy and were pushing forward.

"You men, wait," I said, and Jadoon repeated it.

They responded to my voice and paused, sullenly.

Mirwais spoke, his voice angry and rising. Jadoon said, "Lieutenant Mirwais says that they know what to do."

I ignored them both and turned to greet the jast, Maulana Owir, who had come out to stand in front of his men. He stood very straight, his height emphasised by his pale turban, his face framed by the mandatory dark beard.

"Good morning, Jast. How are you today?" I said, and Wur rendered it in Pashto.

"Good morning, Simon. I have seen that you have not been with the others for a few days. Have you been visiting your own village?" he said.

"Yes, but it's good to be back in the land of light."

"The land of light. Yes, this is the land of light," he said. "Would you care to come and sit and talk with me? I will have tea prepared."

"Thank you, I would be honoured. If you will permit it our doctor would like to practice his skills on anyone you have who may be sick. He could do so while we talk."

The jast nodded and spoke to one of the men behind him in their language, Kamarta Viri.

"And, if you will permit, my men will walk through the village and show the photos again," I said.

"It is not necessary," he said.

"My chief commands it and his chief commands him to command it," I said.

"It is not necessary," he said again, looking at Mirwais. I stood there silently waiting.

"Come then," he said, and turned away.

"Okay, come on Hartigan. Carry on, corporal. You'll know where to find us," I said.

"Yes, sir," Corporal Denton said.

Wur made to go with them but I stopped him.

"I will go and interpret for the search," he said.

"No, Jadoon will go and interpret with the patrol. You'll come and interpret for me," I said.

I followed the jast through the small courtyard, negotiating a stack of rough-hewn timbers and some wooden frames with part-cured goat skins. He walked up a simple ladder to the next level as easily as I would walk up stairs. I followed him up, feeling the ancient timbers give under my heavily laden bulk. When I was up I stood to look around and to wait for Hartigan and Wur to come up behind me.

The village ascended in tiers above us but even at this modest elevation our base was laid out below me. The air was so clean and the light so strong that I felt I could have thrown a stone into it, even though it was at least a quarter of a mile away. Two buildings further on, a couple of ANAs came up to the same level followed by private Higgins. The small gang of brightly clothed children who were squatting on the patio playing with a kitten, called out with shrill voices and a face surrounded by the cloth of a chadri looked out of the doorway. One of the ANAs spoke to her and she came out, reluctantly.

The patio that I was on was covered in square wooden trays and these were covered in fruit drying in the sun; grapes, apricots, walnuts and figs. A young woman was tending them; her slim fingers dexterously turning and sorting them. When I looked at her she paused and looked back at me, curious and fearless. She was much fairer skinned than any of our ANAs, who were all Pashtun from the South.

The heavy, ancient wooden door into the house stood open. This was the biggest house of the village and had the best carving on the doors, window frames and shutters and on some of the main posts that supported the stone and clay infill of the walls. There were intricate basket patterns, rope patterns, flowers, goats and, on a recently replaced shutter, a repeating pattern made of the distinctive shape of the Kalashnikov.

I took the mag out of my SA80, jacked the round out of the chamber, leant it against the wall by the door and squatted down to take off my boots.

"Are you sure, sir?" Hartigan said.

"You'll be safer in there without it, than out here with it, soldier," I said.

"Yes, sir."

Maulana Owir was already seated with a group of long-bearded older men between the four great carved posts that held up the roof. I took the place indicated on the other side of the smouldering fire from him and removed my helmet. Wur squatted to one side. I accepted a bowl of sweet green tea and some lovely, tangy goat's cheese with flatbread. The old men and the jast watched me eat and drink, and when I had finished took up their own bowls of tea and drank.

"Thank you Jast Maulana Owir," I said. "It is nice to be seated again in your beautiful house enjoying this delicious food. May I ask how your affairs have been going since we last met?"

"It is difficult, Simon. The grapes have not been too bad but the wheat has not been so good. And…" He waved his hands in a gentle, circular motion. I noticed that he didn't mention the harvest from the fields of opium poppies.

"And your land is full of outsiders fighting over it and getting in the way?" I said. That brought a grim smile to his face but he didn't respond.

"The Taliban have been quiet of late. Are they preparing to attack the base?" I said.

Maulana Owir looked at Wur. Wur spoke again and it wasn't the same words that he'd used to translate for me.

"What did you say to him?" I said.

"I told him he should answer truthfully," Wur said.

"Don't. Your job is only to translate," I said.

The jast spoke again, his voice firm and angry.

"He says that the Taliban have kept away from the village because you are here," Wur said.

"Excuse me, sir," Hartigan said, from the other side of the room.

He was squatting in the light streaming in from an open shutter. Around him stood or sat a small group of people. A woman was holding the head of a small girl to the light so that he could see her suppurating ear.

"Go and help Hartigan, Wur," I said.

"Thank you, sir," Hartigan said.

The interpreter reluctantly got up and went to translate for the medic, leaving me, the jast and his group of elders looking at one another. The jast gave a command and a girl brought more tea. I accepted it and sipped it, patiently waiting and listening to the faint hiss of the fire and the tone of the words spoken between Hartigan and his patients and Wur.

I had a thought, caught the jast's eye, took a drink of tea and said, "Pi?"

"Pi," he said, nodding.

"Opi," I said, patting my belly and looking happy."

"Opi. Yes, opi," he said, looking clever.

"Yes!" I said, pointing to him. "You speak some English."

"Yes," he said again, smiling.

"What is this?" I said, picking up a knife from the board with cheese on it and holding it up.

"Chaku," he said.

"Chaku?" I said.

He nodded and called out, "Sunik."

The girl who had been sorting dried fruit outside came in and he spoke to her. She nodded her head and then knelt near me and looked at me.

I looked at the jast. "Yes," he said again, waving at her.

"Ah," I said. "My teacher. Thank you."

I pointed to my head and looked the question at the girl.

"She," she said, smiling shyly.

"She," I said.

She pointed to her head and looked at me.

"Head," I said.

"Head," she said.

"Yes!" I said.

"Yes!" she said.

We were all very pleased with ourselves. The girl and I spent a pleasant half-hour teaching each other a few words of our native languages while the jast and his elders looked on with amusement. It was a nice, harmless interlude in an otherwise bad situation.

We were interrupted by shouting. Angry shouting. I got up and ran out onto the patio without ceremony. The jast, Hartigan and Wur were just behind me.

A small group of Jasi men were swarming up the ladder, shouting and looking furious. Every one of them carried an old rifle or an AK. Corporal Denton, several of his men and Jadoon came rapidly up on their heels. The place quickly became crowded. The jast called for silence and there was silence.

"There's been a…" Denton said.

"Wait," I said, holding up my hand to stop him.

I turned to the jast. He nodded and spoke to one of the Jasi men who was most forward of the group. The man fired off a long explanation with passion and gesticulation. When he had finished the jast said a few words to him and then turned to me with a grim face and spoke.

"There has been a fight between Lieutenant Mirwais and some of the people," Wur said.

"He and some of his men robbed one of the houses," Jadoon said.

"I see. Ask the jast if he will allow me to help him judge the matter," I said to Jadoon. "Tell him I respectfully request that we deal with it together."

Wur started speaking to the jast in Pashto.

"Stop," I said and Corporal Denton moved in front of the man, backing him away.

"Go ahead, Jadoon," I said.

Jadoon spoke to the jast. There was some to and fro. Finally Jadoon said, "Yes. He agrees."

"Good. We will follow him to the location," I said, stepping aside and indicating that I would follow Maulana Owir.

"What happened?" I said, sotto voce, to Denton as I quickly laced on my boots.

"Merwas up to his old tricks again, sir. We nearly had a rape as it goes."

"Fuck. Here we go again."

"Yes, sir. Shall I call it in?"

"No, not yet. Let's go see if we can sort this out without disturbing the old man."

We went up through the village, taking narrow paths between houses and ladders to patios and then crossing them to go up again. It was a beautiful, rough but perfect thing, the village, and I wondered if it had ever really known any peace. Perhaps sometimes village life here was much like village life in England, at least in the intervals between invasions. Births, marriages and deaths. Family. I set my face and followed Maulana Owir to the scene of the crime.

Six ANAs including Mirwais, and three rifles were surrounded by a group of Jasi men, all of them armed. Behind them, and on the levels overlooking, there were old and young; most of the village who weren't in the fields, gathered to see. There were more people coming all the time.

We were on a patio in front of one of the smaller houses on the periphery of the village. A woman, an old man and a boy were standing close together at the centre of a group by the entrance to the house. The boy's lip was bleeding. They all looked flushed with anger. Jadoon went to speak to them. Mirwais started talking loudly and gesticulating.

"He says they are Taliban," Wur said. "There was Omar Afridi hiding in their house. He ran away."

"Who was with them?" I said.

"I was, sir," private Grierson said.

"Well?" I said.

"Not that I saw sir, but there could've been. They went in and shut the door before I got there, sir."

"He ran out the back," Wur said.

The boy spoke to the jast, his eyes burning with hatred for Mirwais. Maulana Owir's face became more tense and the mood in the population was turning uglier. The men of the village moved forward and there were words and glances flashing between them.

The ANAs started to huddle together and look scared. The women and elderly moved back through the crowd and now there were at least twenty armed men behind the furious boy.

Mirwais was talking and looking at me.

"They are dirty Taliban," Wur said. "We were only doing our job. You must protect us."

"What have they done, Jadoon?" I said.

"They have taken the family silver," he said, looking at Mirwais.

"What do we do, sir?" Corporal Denton said.

"Hold this," I said, giving him my personal weapon. "And if any ANA raises a gun, shoot him dead."

"Yes, sir."

"Wur, shut up. Jadoon, translate for me," I said, and stepped between the ANAs and the Jasi. Everyone except Mirwais looked at me. He was busy trying to get behind his comrades but they were busy trying to be behind him so it wasn't working.

"The accusation is theft," I said, loudly and Jadoon translated at a similar volume. "What do you say to the charge, Lieutenant Mirwais?"

Mirwais started to speak but I held up my hand to stop him.

"Say it to your accuser," I pointed to the boy and stepped out of the way so that I was no longer between them. This put me beside Mirwais.

"He lies," Mirwais said. "He was harbouring a Taliban. He should be beaten."

The jast looked at me and I looked at him.

"The accused will be searched to prove or disprove the charge," I said. "Do you agree Maulana Owir?"

"Yes," the jast said. "That is good."

There were nods from the crowd. This was going to be entertaining if nothing else.

"It is dishonourable. I will not submit to it," Mirwais said. He started to lift his M16.

"You will," I said, grabbing his gun, continuing the upward motion and taking it out of his hands.

He looked surprised and his eyes followed the rifle as I tossed it to Hartigan. Then he tried to get away but I took hold of his neck. He reached up and tried to get my hands off but it didn't bother me. I squeezed a bit until he stopped struggling and then pushed him forward towards the jast.

"Maulana Owir, will you search him please?" I said. "You could take off his garments one by one."

With great concentration and deliberation the jast began to unbuckle Mirwais's kit, item by item, search and empty them, and lay the contents on the floor.

The backpack, webbing yoke and belt with many pouches and body armour came off. As he emptied each one the jast placed the soldier's legitimate kit in one pile and his thefts in another. There were a heavy pair of earrings, an intricately spiralled torque and a heavy bangle. They were clearly old and of some financial, as well as personal, value. As each piece was laid on the ground for all to see the crowd made an angry sighing sound and pushed forward a little.

Mirwais came back to himself and started struggling again so I subdued him and pushed him down to his knees. Then the jast and I between us stripped him naked including his boots.

"Jadoon, ask someone to go and find a nice whippy branch to beat him with, will you?" I said, "Nothing that'll kill him. Induce them with money and I'll reimburse you later."

"Yes, sir," Jadoon said, and slipped into the crowd. He was good at that; an inoffensive but capable chap Jadoon.

The crowd were looking at Mirwais hungrily, with resentment in their eyes and I knew that his life hung by a thread. Possibly ours too. I stood there, holding my place between the ANA and the Jasi, and waiting. Thankfully they seemed willing to wait with me. I considered using Wur to translate for me but he seemed to have vanished.

Jadoon came back so I said, "Jast, this man would have beaten the boy, let the boy beat him."

"It is not enough," Maulana Owir said. "We will stone him."

"Jast, this man's life is not his own, nor yours, nor mine. He belongs to my commander. If you stone him he will not be fit for duty."

"If we stone him, he will not be fit for life," the jast said.

"I expect Major Snowhall will wish to arrange some compensation for the family and the village," here I gave a slight bow towards him to indicate that by village I meant him personally, "for the insult that they and you have suffered. And to acknowledge your help in resolving this matter without costing him a man."

"This man is of little worth."

"The worth of the man is not his own worth but the worth of his place in his tribe. There is politics in this."

"I will speak to the village."

He moved into the crowd and the senior men huddled round him.

Mirwais tried to make a break for it but Corporal Denton's knee happened to connect with his face in a way that caused him to sit back down. The other ANAs were trying to sidle back out of it but Hesketh and Deaks were in their way.

"We could let them have him, sir," Thompson said, hopefully.

"Was there anyone apart from the family in the house, Grierson?" I said.

"May have been, sir. I thought I saw someone running but I couldn't say who or what, sir."

"We will take this back with us, come what may," I said, indicating Mirwais with the toe of my boot.

"They've decided, sir," Jadoon said.

They had. The jast came to stand in front of me, backed up by the men of the village. Jadoon translated.

"In respect for chief Snowhall we will take the beating and all of his possessions," the jast said.

I looked at the pile of kit. None of it was particularly special but it was army property.

"I'm sure the major would wish to make a better reparation than that tomorrow, Jast," I said. "As I say, this is a man of influence, his life is worth money."

"No. We will settle this now and have it done with."

"Very well, so be it," I said.

The jast spoke to the family and quick hands took up the clothes, and boots and body armour and the webbing with its spare magazines. He himself turned to Hartigan and held out his hand for the M16.

"I'm sorry, Jast. That is not his property, that belongs to the British Army," I said.

He looked pissed off but he accepted it.

I made two ANAs hold Mirwais up and the boy took a maple branch to his back. He was stronger than he looked and he took the job very seriously. The branch was a sturdier item than I'd envisaged too, but there was no helping that. There was quite a bit of screaming and some blood shed by Mirwais. When the boy paused briefly to get his breath back I told the ANAs to carry Mirwais away. They grabbed him, not sure how to hold him, and put him on their shoulders. The crowd hissed in disappointment but no one tried to stop them. I looked for the jast to say goodbye but he had gone.

We left the village followed by many eyes. At the path I called a halt.

"Well done, sir. I thought that was going to kick off," Denton said.

"I was surprised it didn't," I said.

"So was I," Jadoon said.

"Right, six of you come with me. The rest of you can escort this lot home."

They all wanted to come so I chose C section. It was favouritism but I'd know them so much longer than the others and I wanted them, and that was that. Corporal Denton, serious and calm, a rock in any situation. Deaks, with his preferred sharpshooter, class clown and the most likely to say whatever we were all thinking. Thompson, strong as an ox, carrying the gimpy with conscious ease. Hartigan, who would rather stitch a wound than inflict one but who we all knew would do whatever the section needed, whatever it cost him; Milton, youngest of us and in some ways the cleverest; section communications specialist and bearer of the Bowman. And Hesketh, who hadn't quite worked out that she no longer had to prove herself.

We went up and the others went down. When I turned to look back after a hundred yards I saw a figure leave the village and hurry down to join them. Wur had finished whatever piece of larceny he had been up to.

We seven toiled carefully up to the pass above the village. Most of the way it was so stony that nothing could be buried, but wherever there were piles of rock that could hide something Denton went forward to check it out. We kept strung out so that we never presented one target for the enemy and arrived at the top without incident. I left Hesketh settled behind a rock with a view back the way we'd come and took the rest of them over the skyline. I kept Milton with me and the rest separated and sat down in whatever cover there was to rest and watch.

On either side of us the mountains rose to the snow line. At our feet the land fell away steeply to the next valley. Away on the face of the opposing col, a small river, swollen by the snow melting in the strong sunshine, fell into a deep turquoise pool and then rushed down the slope. At the bottom of the valley there was a bridge over the river. The crude but sturdy planks were cantilevered on heavier timbers resting on strong stone buttresses. At some time in the past thousand years or more someone had gone to some trouble to ensure the crossing.

This side of it was Afghanistan; the other side was Pakistan. Unless a mountain goat or an eagle, whatever came in or out of this bit of Nuristan came this way. At the moment I couldn't see anything moving at all. Or not moving for that matter. Now that we had theoretical line of sight I should be able to raise Corporal Johnston on the combat net.

"You there, corp?"

"Third rock from the left, sir."

"Very good. Anything?"

"Not even a goat, never mind any Terry sir."

"Same old story. Never mind. I'll send the lads down a bit to back you up, just in case. We'll call it a day at seventeen forty."

"Seventeen forty it is, sir."

I gave the others the nod to move into position to support the team by the bridge, left Milton near the top to act as a relay for the radios and went back to join Hesketh looking down into our own valley; down towards the base.

"All quiet, sir" she said.

"I don't believe it, Hesketh," I said.

"Me neither, sir."

Below us a string of women and older children in brightly coloured clothes were carrying baskets and wrapped bundles along a path to one of the isolated houses. Below them the patrol base, composed of an uneven triangle of Hesco barriers with tents and improvised buildings inside it, took up a levelish bit of land on a slight rise, flanked on two sides by the winding river.

Almost all around the PB the land dipped towards the river before it rose again to the surrounding mountainsides. It was overlooked for almost three-sixty degrees and you could approach it without being seen for nearly as much. It looked like a regular army fuck-up to me.

"Only bit of level land that wasn't under cultivation I suppose," Hesketh said, reading my thoughts.

The thud of a helicopter beating the air came to us. It was impossible to tell from what direction because the sound was bounced around between the mountains. A Chinook appeared from the direction of Ghanzni, shadowed from above by the sinister shape of an Apache. The Chinook waited at altitude while the Apache carried on over us and disappeared over the ridge of the pass.

"Where's he going?" Hesketh said.

"Having a look see over the border for the old man," I said.

Ten minutes later it came back and kept watch while the ponderous transport chopper set down in the PB, raising a small storm of dust. There would now be dust in places dust were better not. Four men ran out with a stretcher, put it aboard, and it lifted straight up, put its nose down and headed home.

"There goes Lieutenant Mirwais," I said.

"I'll miss him, sir," Hesketh said.

"So will I, Hesketh."

We mused on the departed in silence and then I had another thought.

"Hesketh, where would you put an observation post to give good supporting fire and cover our dead ground?" I said.

"There, sir."

She pointed to a spur of rock that protruded from the shoulder of the mountain that flanked the pass. It commanded a good view of the base and the village and was almost on a level with the pass. There were plenty of shattered sections of stone to give cover too.

"Bit of a scramble," I said.

"Doable, sir."

"Okay, let's do it."

"Sir?"

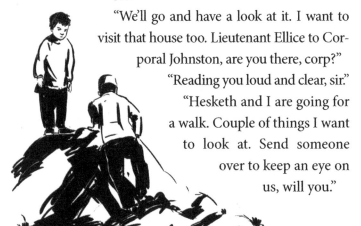

"We'll go and have a look at it. I want to visit that house too. Lieutenant Ellice to Corporal Johnston, are you there, corp?"

"Reading you loud and clear, sir."

"Hesketh and I are going for a walk. Couple of things I want to look at. Send someone over to keep an eye on us, will you."

"Sure you don't want some privacy, sir?"

"Very funny."

"Sorry, sir."

"I'll take the lead, sir," Hesketh said.

"No, Hesketh. You'll come along at a safe distance and walk where I walk."

"Yes, sir."

I picked my way carefully down the slope at an angle until it joined the path that the women and girls had just used. They hadn't been blown up so I decided to use it too. Carefully.

The house was one of those the Nuristani build for partial outcasts; people who have committed adultery or theft and not been wealthy enough to buy their way out of trouble. Anything worse and they were burnt out of their houses and killed or sent away to another part of Nuristan. I had thought it was unused so I was curious to know what the women and children were taking there.

When I got to it, I waited beside the rough stone wall for Hesketh to join me and then we looked in through the open doorway together, rifles raised. Twenty or so chadri framed faces looked at us in alarm. There was a part woven rug taking up most of the floor. Three women were working on it, knitting the wool pattern onto the long warps. Around them women and girls were spinning thread on hand spindles. Most of the floor that wasn't taken up with the rug was piled with their baskets and different coloured mounds of wool. It was an unexpectedly homely, feminine and domestic picture.

We lowered our guns and smiled at them and did our best to look like we meant them no harm. They looked at Hesketh with curiosity, as they almost always did and conversation broke out amongst them.

"Wanted to get away from the men, I expect," Hesketh said, as we carried on towards the spur of rock that was our destination.

"Didn't want to join them then, Hesketh?"

"Fuck off, sir."

There was a steep face of rock to get up and that was bad because we were completely exposed on it and we had to sling our rifles and use both hands. No distant sniper shot me or Hesketh as we made it up and into cover of the rocks. We found ourselves in what was almost a bowl.

Rocks had been piled up around the edges, to make a perfectly serviceable sangar.

There were old 303 casings on the ground. They were tarnished almost to verdigris; whoever had been shooting from here had probably been shooting at Russians, not us.

"Seems like someone else thought so too," I said.

"Wouldn't it be nice to have the HMG up here, sir?" Hesketh said. "No more dead ground."

We looked down at the land around the PB and, I imagine, both swept it through the sights of the oh five oh.

"The OC's right though. It would be a bugger to resupply," I said. "Completely exposed."

"It's been considered, sir?"

"That's one way to put it. And they could come down at us."

I looked up at the ragged boulder-field above us.

"Could cover that with the light gun, sir."

"Or the mortars. Might bring a few rocks down on our heads."

She shrugged as if that were only a minor issue.

"No, that's the problem," I said.

I looked down the way we'd come. There was no getting away from it; getting men and ammunition in and out would be a form of suicide if there were snipers on the other hill.

"That's what darkness is for, isn't it, sir?"

"That, Hesketh, is a good point. You know that?"

"Yes, sir."

I studied the ground around the PB through the glasses. It could have been my imagination but there may have been the faintest signs of a track leading through the scrubby grass of the dead ground to a point in the barrier. Just a hint of line, that's all.

It was too soon to start back down so we sat and waited and watched. A big oblong-shaped raptor glided by hundreds of feet above us and I wondered if it was a Himalayan vulture. Hesketh kept her eyes on the terrain around us.

"I'm sorry about your granddad, sir," she said, out of the blue.

"Thanks," I said.

"It will get better."

"So they say."

"Just don't get kicked out before it does, sir."

"I'm trying not to."

"You're not trying very hard, sir."

"It feels like I am, Hesketh."

"Yes, sir."

Time passed. More women and girls came and went from the house. A hunter came along the track by the river with a mouflon over his shoulder.

"He managed to fit in," I said. "Or at least not get caught."

"Your granddad, sir? In the army?"

"In The Rifles, yes."

"Is he why you joined, sir?"

"He probably is."

"Was he like you?"

"They say so. It's hard for me to tell."

"I'm surprised he managed to stay in then, sir."

"I believe it was a close run thing most of his career. I've no illusions about what he can be like. He can be a selfish, cold-hearted bastard sometimes. So people say anyway, though I've never seen it."

"Good job you didn't turn out like him then, sir."

"Are you taking the piss, Hesketh?"

"No, sir."

The sun would soon touch the flank of the mountain and the temperature would start to drop.

"Could be, I mean," I said.

"I'm sorry, sir."

"Come on then, Hesketh, let's go."

"Time to face the music, sir."

"What music, Hesketh?"

"The ANA's lament, sir."

"Oh, that music."

If you forgot about the whole business of the war it was quite fun sliding down the rock face. I could've been coming down Suliven with Avus. The idea that I couldn't do that again made no sense to me, so I put it away.

We smiled and waved to the women and girls in the house. The edge of the rug where they were working on it had moved on about an inch, revealing a little more of the pattern. They seemed to be packing up for the day too.

We met Corporal Wykham where the paths intersected. They had failed to intercept any insurgents attempting to smuggle munitions into Nuristan. Deaks said something to Hesketh which caused her to kick him in the shin. We made our careful way back to the PB, collecting the team at the bridge on the way. The base was battening down for the night.

I called in at the command post and made my report. The old man wasn't there so I gave Dan Granger the information, such as it was. In our tent Gerald poured a beer in silence and handed it to me.

"That bad?" I said.

"There's a bit of an atmosphere," he said.

I took off my kit with relief and sat on the bed and drank the beer. It was an immensely familiar thing; the tent and the camp bed and the knowledge that I must write up the patrol before it went out of my head and it got even harder to be bothered. I just wanted to lie on the bed and stare at the canvas. And possibly drink another beer.

"You speak, I'll type," Gerald said, opening the ruggedized laptop.

"That may be the nicest thing anyone's ever done for me," I said.

"What, not even Hesketh?"

"Don't you start."

The OC was in the mess with Dan. He didn't make eye contact with us so Gerald and I got our trays and sat at another table. The ANAs were in their usual place but a lot of their usual indolence had gone. They looked at me when I came in and their heads went down so that they could whisper to each other. The major's face was immobile but you could tell that he wasn't a happy bunny.

Gerald and I tucked into our goat stew; comrades in adversity if nothing else.

"Anything interesting occur?" he said.

"That I didn't put in the report?" I said.

"Yes."

"I think I saw a Himalayan vulture."

"But did it see you?"

"They see everything."

"Everyone here sees everything."

"Except where the fuel goes."

"Yes, except that."

We ate in silence for a bit and then he said, "Hang on. Have you got an idea about that?"

"I might have. I suppose the whole camp watched me and Hesketh go up to that old OP."

"Was it an OP?"

"Definitely. Casings from the Russians' time. Nothing recent though."

"Well?"

"Well what?"

"What's your idea?"

"Wait and see."

"Bastard."

It was nineteen thirty. Major Snowhall got up and walked past our table to the exit.

"Come on then, Ellice. Bring your beer," he said.

"Sir."

I followed him to his tent. He was the only one on the base who didn't share.

"Sit."

I sat on the canvas and metal chair. There was a photo of his two daughters on the tea-chest beside his bunk. He poured us both an enamel mug of whiskey from a bottle. I swallowed the last of my beer and accepted the whiskey.

"I suppose you're going to tell me you had no choice?" he said.

"No, sir. I had a choice between pissing off the locals or the ANAs. I chose the ANAs, sir. He stole from that family and would've raped the woman if Grierson hadn't been quick."

"It had to be you though, didn't it."

"Gerald's knackered, sir."

"I know, Ellice. We're all knackered. You supervised a man being beaten half to death."

"I'm sorry, sir."

"No you aren't, Ellice."

There wasn't anything to say to that so I didn't say anything.

"Can you imagine what a shit-storm I'm in over this? We're supposed to be training them to replace us and I send one back beaten to a pulp for heroically doing his duty."

"I saved his life."

"That's not what he's saying. You should have backed up the ANAs and got the hell out of there."

"I thought we were supposed to be win-ning the trust of the local population, sir."

"And that's working, is it?"

"No, sir."

"They've put in a formal com-plaint of brutality and bullying against you and a request not to be instructed or led by you again."

"I'm sorry, sir."

"Don't say that again, Ellice."

"No, sir."

49

"There are calls for an enquiry, damnit. I'm afraid something has to give and you're it. I'm transferring you out."

"I see, sir."

"There's a replacement coming up from Kandahar at fourteen hundred tomorrow and you'll be leaving on his transport. You're confined to base until then."

"I see, sir."

"Under the circumstances, it's hard. I know that, but there it is."

"Yes, sir."

"Now then, while I have you here, I've read your report. No sign of any activity whatsoever. Again. You realise that that's being taken as a justification for this PB? Apparently, we're preventing the flow of weapons into Nuristan."

"If they aren't moving weapons it's because they already have, sir. In my opinion. I'll bet a month's pay they'll move against us within a week, sir."

"If they leave it that long, Ellice. Yes, that's my thought too."

"There was a very fine view from the spur of rock on the north east slope, sir. Perfect field of fire for the HMG."

"Again, Ellice. You're like a dog with a bone. We've been sniped at for three months. How many casualties have we taken?"

"Two, sir."

"Three, including Lieutenant Mirwais. I am not sending men out into such an exposed position while we can have Apaches here in seven minutes. We will keep one hell of a watch, that's all. Understand?"

"Yes, sir."

"You are confined to base. That's a direct order."

"Yes, sir."

"You don't seem to get this, Ellice, but this is my command and these men are my responsibility. That means I get to decide how we play it. Understand?"

"Yes, sir."

"Go back to your duty. That will be all, Ellice."

"Thank you, sir."

I gave him back his empty mug and went out into the dust of the compound and walked towards my tent. The last of the light was hanging on the highest peaks and it would be full dark in a few minutes. A likely time for enemy action.

"You alright, sir?" Thompson said, at the mortars.

"Fine thank you, Thompson," I said.

"Enjoyed the bimble today, sir."

"Good."

"Nice to have you back, sir."

"Eyes peeled, Thompson."

"Yes, sir."

There isn't much in the way of privacy in a patrol base. I didn't want to walk round the defences yet and be reminded of what else I was losing, so I went back to my tent and lay on my bunk and got on with the staring at the canvas that I'd wanted to do earlier.

Gerald found me there and said, "Fuck, Si. I just heard. I'm sorry."

"Can't blame him. Not much else he could do."

"C section are going to be gutted."

"They'll get over it."

"Yes, but…"

"You'll all have things to take your mind off it soon enough."

"You think that'll help? You're wrong you know. That's when they'll really miss you. I will too."

"Shut up, Ger."

"Sorry."

"Maybe it'll be tonight. First light, I mean," I said.

"I almost wish it would be. Get it over with."

"Me too."

"Tell you what, distract yourself and me with your idea, will you?"

"What idea?"

"About the fuel, for fuck's sake."

"Oh okay, why not. Where are the ANAs right now?"

"Some are on stag, if you can call it that. I think the rest are getting up a game of Buzkashi on the parade ground."

"I thought you needed horses for that?"

"They're riding each other."

"What are they using as a goat?"

"Private Barbar. I think he's also the prize."

"Poor sod. That'll do. Come with me."

"Anywhere, Si."

"Fuck off."

I led him towards the shithouse and diverted behind the supplies tent. We were between it and the Hesco barriers here and it was an unconsidered space of things dumped; unloaded pallets, unwanted chests, empty containers. There were three layers of the massive gravel-filled bags beside us; smaller ones on bigger ones; enough height to protect the more sensitive components of the base, like the accommodation, from plunging fire from the mountains.

"You think they get it over here?" Gerald said.

"Not over, no," I said.

I got out my torch and studied the footprints in the dust, walking slowly forward.

"What're we looking for?" Gerald said.

"Boot prints going nowhere. Like these." I pointed.

"If you say so."

We quietly lifted three empty pallets out of the way. Some rocks protruding from the ground meant that the Hescos hadn't sat down quite level and there was a gap; nothing that would let anything bigger than a rat in, but enough to feed a length of plastic tube through. There was a funnel sitting nearby.

"Well, fucking hell," Gerald said.

"Why don't we wedge a flashbang under the pallets and leave it be?" I said.

"Tempting, but I think we'll just quietly tell Dan. He'll be over the moon."

"That is why I'm getting transferred and you're not," I said.

"In a nutshell, Si. Yes. You idiot. Sometimes I think you want to get kicked out."

We put the pallets back and made a discreet withdrawal. Gerald wanted us to go straight to the 2IC but I opted to make my rounds of the defences instead so he went on and I walked to the main sangar and climbed the ladder. Hartigan and a soldier called Jones, who I didn't really know, were on watch behind the barrier of sandbags. It was fully dark now. The low roof obscured the sky above but the gap between its edge and the ragged line of the mountains was filled with bright stars.

"They're really kicking it up tonight, sir," Hartigan said.

"Are they?"

"Look for yourself, sir."

He handed me the glasses and I looked.

The village's dance floor was on one of the higher terraces where the configuration of the land and the houses had combined to give a large expanse of patio. There was an unusually generous fire blazing and figures moved in front of it. Yes, they were partying tonight. I wondered why. As I watched, music started, carrying clearly in the still air; a high, urgent chant on something that sounded like a flute, backed by tabor and then some kind of stringed instrument. It was wild and simple and suited the place and the atmosphere well.

"Didn't invite us then, sir," Hartigan said.

"No. Don't get cold. I'll see you later," I said, and left them to go on round.

The ANAs were supposed to be helping with the watch but their presence only annoyed the men so everyone connived at letting them slope off it as much as possible. Hesketh and Thompson were cradling steaming mugs of hot chocolate beside the light gun, the long finger of its barrel pointing at the hillside from where snipers had operated previously.

"You let it happen, sir," Hesketh said, unable to keep the resentment out of her voice.

"I couldn't help it, Hesketh," I said. "I'm sorry."

"So am I, sir. So are we all."

"When will you be back, sir?" Thomson said.

"I don't know that I will. I don't know what's going to happen to me."

"I wish you sounded like you cared, sir," Hesketh said.

"C section won't like it, sir," Thompson said.

"They will have to lump it, as I will," I said.

"You have to do something, sir. This is crap and you know it," Hesketh said.

"There's nothing I can do, Hesketh."

"That's just no good, sir. You wouldn't take that from any of us."

"Just keep your watch, soldier."

I turned to go, ignoring the hurt I was causing. It was just a small reflection of the hurt I was feeling.

I looked in at the other watch stations briefly, just to see all was well but not to get into conversation, and went to the comms shack. Signaller Hardcastle was at the set, big olive headphones obscuring much of his head. He nodded to me and went back to concentrating. I checked the screen showing the thermal image sensors that looked out into the night; nothing warm-blooded was moving on the hills, and pulled up a chair. The temperature was dropping and I wished I'd thought to go and get myself some hot chocolate before I came in.

An hour later I rectified that after I'd walked round again and got some for Hardcastle too. There was a light on in the OC's tent. He never seemed to sleep, poor sod; carrying the whole thing on his back. Two hours after that Gerald tapped me on the shoulder and I went off to our tent.

I took off my body armour, helmet and boots and lay under my sleeping bag on my cot staring at the canvas. I wanted to sleep but I kept thinking about Avus and then trying not to think about him and all the things we would no longer be able to do together. I got the old pipe of his that I'd lifted from the desk in his study out of my pocket and sniffed it and rubbed the polished wooden bowl with my fingers. Ironic that it was his and precious to me, and that it had almost certainly helped to take him from me.

An hour later I'd moved on to thinking about C section and some of the others and wishing I didn't have to leave them. And to wishing I'd thought to have a piss before lying down. I didn't bother to put my boots on but just walked through the tents to use the side of the barriers as many did. A light cloud covering had obscured the stars and it was bloody dark so I went by touch as much as by sight.

I was standing there smelling the warm pungent smell rising from the stream of liquid hitting the wall and listening to the distant beat of the music that was still coming from the village when I heard a sound that was something between a grunt and a sigh and then a low, persistent scuffling. I zipped myself up and went in search of its source, treading silently on the packed dirt.

It was really black dark back there and I don't think I was fully awake. I caught my foot on one of the sandbags holding down the bottom of a tent and then tried to catch myself against the canvas and banged my hand into it instead. It wasn't much noise but it was enough. I heard feet hurrying away and turned on my torch and went forward quickly.

Wur was lying face down and I could see from the marks on the ground that it had been his feet that had made the scuffling sound.

He was firm and unresponsive to the touch, as the dead are, and had no detectable pulse in his neck. A hand over his mouth and a long blade up under his ribs unless I was mistaken. I turned him over.

One of his open eyes had particles of dirt in it and that more than the blood and lack of pulse said that he was dead. I squatted over him, listening. I wished I'd brought my sidearm but there were no sounds of movement. I went through his pockets, collecting two phones, a few papers, some money in different currencies and a dangerous looking knife, and then left quietly and went back to my tent.

There was some writing on one of the papers. It looked like a list but I couldn't read it. The phones had a few numbers stored in them but not under any names. There were some texts but, again, not in a language I could read.

I sat on the bed and stared into the darkness for a bit. Then I got out the old pipe and sniffed it again and stroked it for a bit. Life, apparently, is finite.

I took my socks off and beat them against the leg of the cot to get any dirt off them and then put them and my boots back on. I suited up, put my helmet on, made sure I had night vision, spares mags for my SA80 and went out.

Our two interpreters, suiting their ambiguous position, shared a tent between our tents and the ANAs. I tapped on the pole at the entrance and went in. Jadoon was in bed, his sleeping bag pulled up to his chin. I put a hand on his shoulder and shook him gently. He opened his eyes and looked at me.

"Hi, Jadoon. Are you awake?" I said.

"I am now," he said.

"Sorry. Could you just read this for me?"

"Read what?"

"This."

I pulled the piece of paper out of my pocket. He put a hand out from under the covers and took it. His eyes widened when he saw it and then he got control of his expression.

"Something interesting?" I said.

"Just a list of money owed I think. There are names of some of the ANA and figures."

"Okay, thanks."

I made to take it, but he kept it and said, "I'll transcribe it for you in the morning."

"Not to worry, I'm sure it's not important."

I took hold of his wrist in one hand and the paper in the other.

"Let go, Jadoon, or we'll tear it," I said.

"If you wish," he said, and let go.

"Thanks. Sorry I woke you. See you in the morning."

"Yes, sir," he said.

As I walked across the parade ground towards the light gun my mind noticed that Jadoon's boots hadn't been under his cot.

Hesketh and Thompson were still on duty there.

"Hi, you two," I said, sitting down next to them.

"Couldn't sleep, sir?" Hesketh said.

"Something like that," I said.

"You alright, sir?" Thompson said.

"Just thinking," I said.

"Oh."

They let me think for a bit and then Hesketh said, "Anything we can do, sir?"

"You must be off in a minute, Hesketh?" I said.

"Yes, sir. Five minutes now."

"It's very dark out there, isn't it?"

"Very dark, sir."

"I've got a feeling, Hesketh," I said.

"Have you, sir?"

"Yes. I fancy a walk up to that place we were at today. Do you think C section would like to stretch their legs?"

"Yes, sir, I'm sure they would," she said, sitting up and looking happy.

"But, sir..." Thompson said.

"Shut up, you idiot," Hesketh said.

"Need to make sure all watch stations are covered, though," I said.

"Leave it to me, sir," she said.

"And I think we'll go with a gimpy, Thompson," I said.

"I was going to get one, sir."

"We might be up there for a while."

"Ratpacks all round, sir."

"Okay. Rendezvous behind the stores tent at oh five hundred."

"We'll be there, sir."

I gave them a smile, and in doing so, realised that it had been a long time since I'd smiled last.

It was a heavily loaded section that assembled under the Hescos behind the stores tent. I'd been kneeling there with my sig in my hand watching through the helmet mounted night vision system but no one had come to bother me.

They came silently, one by one, and knelt beside me, automatically taking up positions to observe. Like me they had night vision on and this obscured much of their faces but I was certain that they were happy to be up to something at last. It was a good feeling to have them around me once more.

"Right, you lot. I think I know the path but I could be wrong. Any loud noises and you go right back to bed and pretend this never happened. Got it?"

"Got it, sir."

"If at all possible, all the NV kit needs to get back. Understand?"

"Materiel of tactical significance, sir," Denton said.

"Yes. We'll pause at the edge of dead ground for me to have a chat with Lieutenant Page and then we go on up. Hesketh knows the way so if you aren't following me, follow her."

"You could just borrow our tent, sir," Deaks said.

"Permission to punch him, sir?" Hesketh said.

"Later, Hesketh. Now, we don't know if we're poking a hornets' nest so we'll have Thompson and Hesketh hanging back to lob in some forty mils if we make contact. Radio silence, everyone. Ready?"

Nod and thumbs up all round.

"Come on then."

Denton gave me a boost up and I went over, keeping flat on the top so that I showed the minimum profile. I let myself down. No loud bangs. I had a look round and saw only grass and a pair of mouflon grazing it in the greenish intensified image. They put their heads up and looked at me. It was good to know that they were there; a cloven hoof will set off an IED as easily as a regulation army boot.

I leant my SA80 against the wall and waved Denton down, steadying him as he dropped. As each man came down he automatically took up watch with his weapon raised. Thompson passed down the general purpose machine gun to me and then came down and we were all there.

I could see where men had stood to fill cans from the protruding stub of plastic pipe and when I squatted down and concentrated I could follow the line in the grass which was the path. I led off without word and they followed at intervals.

The mouflon watched us go but didn't yield any ground.

The path was on soil; an easy place to bury an IED, so I just had to trust that this wasn't a trap. I made it to the river shore which was bedrock and gravel and waited for Denton to come up. He would be a way-marker until the next man came. I went on again, not towards the bridge and the village, but away from it. When I reached the spot that I'd identified earlier I waited again and then walked into the river. It was cold enough to make me catch my breath and deeper than I'd hoped. I forged on, my feet slipping on the smooth boulders. If I fell in it would be a real bugger.

We went on like this, spread out, dot and carry one, me leading and Hesketh in the middle, until we were on the shoulder of the opposite mountain and below the old Observation Post that we'd visited earlier in the day. No one shot at us and none of us stood on an IED. So far so good. I flicked on my comms system and spoke over the combat net.

"Lieutenant Ellice to Lieutenant Page. Come in Gerald, if you're there."

"What the fuck, Si? Why are you on the combat net? You're in bed, aren't you?" Gerald said. He seemed to be whispering.

"Not exactly. Are you by the IR?"

"Am as it happens. Why? Where are you?"

"You're about to see a few people emerge from the dead ground and start ascending the hill, north-north-east. It's me and C section. Perhaps you could refrain from killing us."

"Si…"

"And I won't be offended if you tell the old man.

You've got a future to protect."

"I'm afraid…"

"He's standing behind you?" I said.

"Return to base, Ellice. That is an order," Snowhall's voice said.

"I believe it's coming, sir. First light I expect," I said.

"I've had the drones fly over again and there's nothing moving. I repeat, nothing moving. Return to base."

"Sorry, sir."

I switched off.

It was Denton who disturbed the first rock. It bounded down the slope making an appalling noise. Except it probably wasn't as bad as I thought; mouflon must do the same thing and I've never heard one. We stared up at the lip of piled stone above us. No one started shooting. No lights came on. No grenade tumbled down to us.

"On me," I said, and went up fast, my rifle slung on my back.

Deaks and Hartigan were with me. I put my head up. Empty. I scrambled in and helped them up.

"Thank fuck for that," I said.

"My grollies are frozen stiff, sir," Deaks said. "That water was very fucking cold."

"Mine too, Deaks," I said, waving the others up. "But unlike yours, mine are in for a roasting when we get back."

"Rosy fingered dawn," I said.

The high cloud had softened the light, and the new day was breaking in pink.

"Did she, sir?" Hesketh said.

"Night's candles are burnt out and jocund day stands tiptoe on the misty mountain tops," I said.

"You're an unusual kind of rupert sometimes, sir," Deaks said. "No offence intended."

"None taken. We must have bloody noses and crack'd crowns and pass them current too. God's me, my…"

"Are you alright, sir?" Denton said.

"Don't mind him, corp," Hesketh said. "He gets like this sometimes."

"… horse, I think," I said.

"It's getting light, sir," Denton said.

"Eyes sharp everyone," I said.

"By the way, what are we doing here, sir?" Deaks said. "I don't care like, but I was just wondering. Why today?"

"Do you know what I think?" I said.

"Not usually, sir," Hartigan said.

"I think Wur was green slime."

"Was, sir?"

"Yes, was. I found him behind the stores tent earlier. I think Jadoon and a couple of ANAs killed him and I think it means it's all about to kick off."

"Well fuck me, I'd never of guessed," Hesketh said.

Below us in the base there was a sharp crack and the

signals hut collapsed in on itself. Armed men streamed out of the mosque and ran to cross the river at the bridge and at a shallow place downstream of it. As they neared the barriers a heavy machine gun opened up from the house below us.

"You were right, sir," Denton said.

"Comms on. Engage the enemy," I said.

Thompson started working with the gimpy, trying to stop the tide of men surging over the barriers and Deaks was pinging away with his sharpshooter. Those of us with SA80s held our fire; out of effective range. Our turn would come later. The machine gun in the house was keeping up steady, disciplined fire at the watchtowers and there wasn't much in the way of return fire coming back.

"RPGs," I said.

"See them," Thompson said.

The puffs of smoke indicating the launch of RPGs came from several points on the top of the barriers and there were detonations at the mortar positions and light gun. And then further detonations as ammunition went up.

"Shit."

Men were running inside the base. Some towards the Command room and some towards the entrance. The ANAs streamed out of the entrance and took shelter behind the Hescos.

"Lieutenant Ellice calling zero, come in. Over."

Nothing.

"Lieutenant Ellice to call-sign zero, are you reading me? Over."

"Shit. Try to raise them on the VHF, Milton."

"She's getting hot, sir," Thompson said.

"Keep going," I said.

Hartigan was feeding belt after belt to the gimpy and men were falling from the barriers. Then they were running: running away from the base, back towards the shelter of the mosque.

"Rest it, Thompson," I said. "You keep going, Deaks."

"Sir."

"No answer, sir," Milton said.

"Bastards. I think they've taken out the light gun and the mortars too. I'm not sure about the javelins," I said.

I was searching the base through my glasses. I could see bodies at the mortar emplacements and one man was crawling slowly towards the shelter of the command post. He was having to drag his legs behind him. The long finger of the light gun had dropped out of sight, which wasn't a good sign. The canteen tent had smoke billowing out of it. At least everyone apart from the crawling man was into cover.

There were a number of bodies on the top of the PB's wall. As I watched, someone inside the command post shot a man who was trying to crawl back over the wall and he slumped down and was still. I counted twenty or so dead in the area between the mosque and the base. Good shooting by Thompson.

An RPG curved out from near the mosque, cleared the Hesco wall and exploded in the parade ground, doing no harm.

Beside me Denton put a burst at the house below us and two men with AKs ran back into cover.

"She's ready, sir," Thompson said.

"Keep their heads down but conserve your rounds. I don't suppose help is on the way. How many Terrys do we think we're dealing with anyone?"

"A lot, sir," Denton said. "Two hundred at least and look, sir."

He pointed to the village. I put the glasses on it. The light was strengthening every minute and what had just been dark spaces were becoming visible. There were more people there than I expected and they didn't seem to be villagers. There was a group at the place where the partying had been. They were looking in our direction and there was something else…

"Deaks."

"On it, sir."

He moved to the edge of the space facing the village and pushed his sharpshooter into the gap between two stones.

There was a flash of light, quickly subdued by pale smoke and then the crack of detonation.

"Incoming."

I watched the heavy, blunt anti-tank missile rise and rise and then begin to fall, seemingly slow but then suddenly very fast.

It hit fifty yards short of us and more than that to the right. Splinters of rock flew up to us and the ground shook a bit.

Deak's gun chattered and the men round the recoilless rifle in the village ran for cover. Not all of them though, three at least wouldn't run again.

Below us the heavy machine gun in the house was pecking away at the base. Not wasting ammunition but keeping them bottled up. As I looked at it with my glasses a man was looking at me with his, peering carefully round the doorway. Down at the foot of the village men with AKs ran out and began to work up towards us. There was some small arms fire coming up to us, none of it well aimed.

"Right," I said. "They can't get into the base while we're here so they'll want to dislodge us as quickly as possible. We're all going to die if we don't get help so Milton, you get up high enough to bounce a signal over to Ghanzni and call in the uglies. Corporal Denton, you go with him, distract anyone who tries to stop him and take over if necessary?"

"Yes, sir."

"Thompson and Hartigan, you see to it that no one crosses from the mosque to the base. Deaks, kill whoever you can see."

"Yes, sir."

"Hesketh, you and I will nip down the hill and winkle out that HMG."

"Will we, sir?"

"Yes. Hopefully they'll be so interested in us they won't notice Denton and Milton going out the back. Ready, everyone?"

"Ready, sir."

"Go."

Thompson and Deaks did what they could to provide us with covering fire and Hesketh and I rolled out of the OP at the front and went down the initial bare rock slope, sliding and scrambling down at the risk of broken bones. A few bullets sang off the rock but we were still out of effective range of all the enemy except those in the house below us. When we got to cover in the broken ground below I looked back and caught a glimpse of Denton and Milton climbing like monkeys through the boulders above the OP and then the curve of the land hid them.

"Moving," I said, and started working forward while Hesketh went firm and put suppressive fire at the house. I got to some kind of cover behind a rock and took my turn while she leapfrogged me. Two men ran from the house and I tried for them but they got into cover before I could catch up with them.

"Covering," Hesketh said

"Moving," I said, and ran for it.

We went down the slope fast. There was more fire coming at us now and from different angles; they'd managed to get men out away from the house and into the cover of the folds of the slope and the piles of rocks. This meant that it was becoming impossible to keep their heads down while we moved. As we closed them we were coming more and more into effective range of their AKs. It was a game we were more likely to lose the longer it went on.

Above us Thompson and Hartigan were working the gimpy constantly. A flash of movement caught my eye and then there was a tremendous crump. I didn't stop to see but ran again.

"Covering."

No answer. I was in effective grenade range now so I used the underslung launcher on my SA80 to put one somewhere near the door of the house and then one in the rocks into which I'd seen men run.

"Hesketh. Come in, Hesketh."

No response.

No time. I finished that mag, swopped in another and ran forward. Men came out of the house, raising their AKs. I went down into a firing position on my knees; they were in the SA80's comfortable range now and they weren't wearing body armour. Time slowed down. I narrowed my attention on the one to the right, bones, muscles, breathing coming into alignment. One, two.

His body bucked as both rounds went in. A bullet from his AK rose and fell towards me in the 4X sight even as I was tracking left. No time to think about that.

The next man, a white tunic, his AK stuttering, held badly, centre mass, there. One, two.

One in at least, the man falling sideways, his gun still firing. Moving left.

Something tugged at my head.

No time.

A man pulling out the mag, bending over it. Centre mass. One, two. Falling back. Got him.

No cover. No time. The sound of an AK from my right.

I ran. It's not so easy to hit a moving target with an AK at more than a hundred meters. The angle of my run was bringing the doorway of the house into view. A man leant against the frame and took deliberate aim at me.

I threw myself down onto the stony ground, fumbling for another grenade. His bullets were passing over my head. I got it into the launcher, closed it and made myself adjust the sights.

He saw me aiming and ducked back in. The round-headed forty mill lump of high explosive followed him in and there was the sharp detonation. The heavy machine gun stopped firing.

I pulled a splinter of rock from my hand and sucked the wound. Behind me there were shots: an SA80. I looked back. Nothing to see. Down-slope two men got up from the slight cover of a depression and ran. They ran away, leaping and skidding like chamois, their guns held high to help them balance.

More shots from an SA80.

"Hesketh? Is that you, Hesketh?"

"Sir? Bloody hell, sir."

I found her wedged between two rocks. There was blood running down her right leg and she wasn't normally conscious. When I cut the cloth away it was bright red, arterial. I bound some gauze over it, checked her for other damage and put in one dose of morphine.

Another anti-tank missile passed over us and hit near the OP. The gimpy was still firing though. On the ground between us and the village men were moving. As I watched some made it over the skyline of the pass. Others were working closer, using what cover the terrain provided. There were a lot of them.

"I think we'd better get moving," I said.

"Sir?"

"Let go of your weapon, Hesketh. This may hurt a bit."

"Sir?"

I took it out of her hands, slipped out the magazine and tossed it away. Then I lifted her onto my shoulder. She groaned a bit and tried to help.

"Come on then. Let's go see what we've done," I said.

No reply.

I couldn't manage better than a stumbling walk down to the house but no one bothered us. There was more smoke rising from the base. The air was full of the brittle sounds of small arms fire and still, the heavier burr of the gimpy above us. Thompson must surely be out of ammunition soon.

I put her against the wall and stepped into the house. The grenade had done most of its work low down, shattering the men's legs. One was clearly dead. I dispatched another as he tried to lift his AK and gave the last one, one to the head to be sure. He looked familiar. The DSh-Ka 12.7ml Soviet heavy machine gun at the window seemed to be undamaged.

Back outside I checked the men there and tapped one whose arm twitched.

"How're you doing, Hesketh?"

"The sun's nice, sir."

"Think you could feed a belt?"

"Of course, sir."

There was no window facing the village or the slope above, so I heaved the Dushka out and put it on the path beside the house. There were baskets stacked on the half-finished rug, the baskets the women had been carrying the day before. Each one held a neatly folded belt for the gun. I carried some outside and put them beside it, marvelling at the weight the women had carried without showing it.

"Do you think they'll let you stay after this, sir?" Hesketh said.

"I'm not sure anyone'll be staying after this. At this rate there may not even be an after. What do you think?"

"I think the uglies will come, sir."

I forced open the top of the gun and had a look. A

miss-fire was stuck in the breach, so I heaved on the cocking mechanism to get it out. That belt was nearly done so I disengaged it and threw it to one side.

"You look happy, sir."

"You know what, Hesketh?"

"What, sir?"

"I am feeling better."

"Me too, sir. Sort of."

I started a new belt, slammed home the cover and heaved on the cocking handle again. It sounded and felt okay.

"You know you have to grieve, sir?"

"What's that?"

"You have to grieve, sir."

"Do I?"

"Yes. Anger won't do."

"Oh. I didn't know that."

"He may be dead but you can still ask him what to do, sir."

"Yes, I know that."

"I think you're going to be okay, sir."

"I didn't think so, but you may be right."

"I don't think I'm going to be okay though, sir."

"You're pretty tough, Hesketh."

"Not your fault, sir. Wouldn't have missed it for the world."

"Ready?"

"Always, sir."

I picked her up as carefully as I could and put her beside the gun. She nearly passed out but she held on. The small arms fire was nearing the OP and several men with RPG tubes were moving up behind the leaders. They would be at almost point blank range soon.

"I'm here, sir," she said, taking hold of the belt.

"Okay. Here goes nothing."

I gripped the two wooden handles, swung the gun on its short tripod and looked through the sight. The lever was smooth under my finger. I braced and squeezed. The gun came alive, its heavy mechanism hammering metallically, the belt feeding smoothly and half inch jacketed rounds smashing into the rocks a quarter of a mile away. The heavy percussion of the exploding propellant deafening us and beating the gun back into my braced body. I adjusted my aim and started to work the gun. On the slope men were running like rabbits. A badly aimed RPG sailed over us and burst behind the house. Long distance AK fire was singing off the rocks all over the place.

Partway through the second belt Hesketh thumped me on my shoulder. I let go of the lever and looked at her.

"Uglies," she said.

I looked up. The lumpy, disfigured fish shape of an Apache helicopter swam overhead and I realised that the air was full of the wump of its rotors.

"Do you think they know we're here, sir?" Hesketh said.

"Oh shit. ISAF ground force to Apache, come in. Over… ISAF ground force to Apache, come in. Over…"

The valley was full of Apaches and it was starting to rain canon-fire and anti-personnel cluster munitions.

I scooped her up and ran for the house. Around us the air began to roar and sizzle.

She died in the under-croft where they'd stored the Dushka while everything around us turned to fire and darkness. I didn't know until the Apaches stopped trying to kill us and ceased fire. I was holding her tight against me and I didn't know that she'd gone.

When the ground stopped shaking and it was only dust and falling particles in the air I eased her away from me and said, "Hey, Hesketh. You were right, I do want to live."

She settled back onto the dirt and my finger couldn't find a pulse and I could feel no breath from her lips.

There was nothing to do so I pushed my way out of the rubble and waved at the nearest ugly. It came over to look, cannons swivelling towards me. I tapped my head and started to call it over the combat net.

Later, when we'd established communication and I'd been able to tell them the probable locations of the rest of C section I hunted in the rubble for the souvenir I wanted, found it, and then walked down to the base. Hesketh could stay where she lay for now.

Two Chinooks delivered reinforcements and started taking away the casualties. One Apache hovered overhead, keeping watch, and the others searched the hillsides.

Major Snowhall was sitting outside the remains of the ops room directing the evacuation of his men and refusing to let the medic attend to him yet. Men were running here and there in purposeful activity. The dead had already been laid out in a row under a tarp. There didn't seem to be more than a handful.

"Si!" Gerald said, coming out of the building with an armful of comms kit.

"Hi, Ger. You made it then," I said.

"Not a scratch. I can't believe you're still alive."

"I seem to be," I shrugged.

"Is that what I think it is?"

"This?" I held up the thing in my left hand.

"Fuck!"

"Present for the old man. Omar Wardak was here. He was directing operations from that house on the hillside."

"That explains a lot."

"Indicators? What indicators, exactly?" Lt. Col. Harrison of Intelligence said back at Ghanzni.

"There was the fact that the local man refused the offer of money tomorrow in preference for a few minor possessions at the time. Followed by all the noise during the night. We assumed that was to cover the movement of forces. And then the women moving things to the house."

"So Major Snowhall decided to risk sending a section out undercover of darkness?"

"Yes, just in case. To an observation point which had already been reconnoitred and found not to be in use by the insurgents, yes, sir. The OC suspected that the absence of low level activity indicated the presence of a serious player like Wardak, sir."

"Altogether a remarkable piece of foresight under the circumstances."

"A very wise decision on his part, sir."

"Yes indeed. A shame we didn't know about Jadoon."

"It's a complex situation out here, sir."

"Isn't it."

He didn't believe me, but he couldn't see what was wrong. It was a plausible story, and no one was contradicting it.

"May I ask what you've found out, sir?"

"Yes, under the circumstances you're entitled to know."

He filled in some gaps for me. I'd been right, Wur had been with them. He'd organised the smuggling out of the fuel in order to establish good relations with the locals. Perhaps he'd got wind of what was coming; we'd never know. It was Jadoon who had taken out the comms room and Jadoon wasn't the Jadoon his papers had said he was, now that someone had bothered to check him out properly.

They found the cave at the back of the village where the munitions had been stockpiled and where the enemy had gathered and waited, each man with a thermal blanket to shield his heat signature from the eyes in the sky. Maulana Owir and many of the men and boys of the village had died too; fighting for a cause that wasn't theirs; caught between us and the Taliban.

They found some of the bodies of the ANAs but most of them just vanished like smoke. Casualties amongst the Rifles had been relatively light considering; only six dead in the base.

And then of course there was C section.

It was Corporal Denton who got the radio up high enough; taking it from Milton's body and harassed all the way up by lighter, fitter, more acclimatised Afghans. He died still sending; calling it in instead of defending himself.

Hartigan and Thompson took a direct hit from an RPG into the OP just before I opened up with the Dushka. If I'd been a little quicker they would have made it.

Deaks had moved out of cover to try and flank the Terrys attacking the OP and died in friendly fire from the Apaches cleaning up.

"All in all, it could have been a much bigger fuck up," Harrison said. "There'll be some brag rags handed out unless I'm much mistaken."

"Posthumously," I said.

"In the main, yes. Your OC wants to talk to you, by the way, Ellice."

"Thank you, sir."

"Good luck, Ellice. I expect I'll be seeing you."

I found Major Snowhall in the Rec Room and we adjourned to a quiet table with a bottle of whiskey and two glasses. He looked tired and defeated.

"You were right," he said, pouring me some. "Without you on the high ground we would all have died."

"So were you," I said. "I got C section killed."

"Yes, you did."

I drank some whiskey and thought about the others. Denton, Thompson, Hartigan, Deaks, Milton and Hesketh. Mainly Hesketh.

"Why did you do it?" he said. "When you found Wur you should've brought it to me. We'd have posted sentries."

"I didn't think you'd listen. It wouldn't have been enough anyway. You wouldn't have taken the risk."

"I might have. If I'd known."

"Anyway, I didn't care. I wanted to prove you wrong."

"Well, you did that."

"And I wanted to stay. I didn't want to be separated from C section. I've been with them since the beginning. Did you know that?"

"No, I didn't. That worked out for you then."

I looked at him and he averted his eyes.

"Sorry, that was crass."

"I'm not hiding from the fact I got them killed," I said.

"Well you did. Was it worth it?"

"Truthfully?"

"You might as well."

"Yes, I think it was."

"You're a sick bastard. You know that?"

I shrugged.

"I suppose I may be," I said. "I believe it runs in the family."

He looked at me as if I were another species; incomprehensible and offensive. I drank some of his scotch and looked at him. It struck me just how little I cared what he thought.

"You disobeyed a direct order," he said. "I can have you court marshalled."

"I saved your arse. Sir," I said.

"I won't let you do it again."

We drank some more scotch. It wasn't a friendly silence, but it was a truthful one.

"The Desmonds might have you," he said.

"I don't think I want the army in any form," I said. "Write me up as temperamentally unsuited and let me go."

"I haven't the first idea what the fuck you are suited to."

"So? Will you?"

"That easy, huh?"

"Unless you've got a better idea?"

"What will you do?"

"Go and visit their families."

"And say sorry?"

"No, I'll tell them how brave and loyal and wonderful they were."

"Why?"

"Because they would appreciate it. And it's true. And I owe them."

He looked at me like I was a piece of shit again.

"And after that?" he said.

"After that I'll go to sea and do my grieving. See if I can sail myself to the other side of it."

When I walked out to the waiting chopper that would take me away, the hard light and the dust were the same as they'd been before, but I wasn't quite the same. As the bird lifted off, I took Avus's old pipe out of my pocket and sniffed it and stroked it one last time. Then I tossed it into the rotor-wash and it was instantly gone.

GLOSSARY

2IC – second in command.

Af – Afghani, the currency of Afghanistan.

ANA – Afghan Nation Army.

Avus – Latin for grandfather.

Bimble – to wander about.

Brag rags – medal ribbons.

Buzkashi – Central Asian game. Usually played on horseback. The object of the game is to get the carcass of a goat or similar into the goal.

Combat net – combat network radio.

Desmonds – SAS/SBS.

Fifty cal – fifty calibre machine gun. Fifty calibre is half an inch.

Forty mils – forty millimetre grenades.

Gimpy – general purpose machine gun.

Green slime – military intelligence.

Hesco wall/barrier – massive square sandbags piled on top of each other. The Hesco system was originally devised for flood control as well as fortification. A digger fills the bags with gravel, or whatever is available locally, and piles them up to form protective barriers as needed.

HMG – heavy machine gun.

IED - Improvised explosive device.

IR – infrared thermal imaging system.

Jast – Afghan head-man.

Javelin – shoulder launched, anti-armour, fire and forget missile system.

KBM – named after the Russian K. B. Mashinostroyeniya armaments factory this refers to a common Soviet shoulder mounted anti-aircraft weapon.

Light Gun – 105mm Howitzer.

OC – officer commanding. The officer in command of a force not big enough to warrant the title commanding officer.

OP – observation post.

PB – patrol base.

QRF duty – Quick Reaction Force. Sitting around in full kit waiting while nothing happens, usually.

Ratpack – field rations.

RPG – rocket propelled grenade.

Rupert – officer.

SA80 – current standard British Arm assault rifle.

Sangar – temporary fortification, originally constructed of stones and earth but now usually of sandbags, tin sheet and similar. The word is originally Persian and came into the British Army through its use by the British Indian Army.

Sharpshooter – L129A1 Sharpshooter Rifle.

Stag – guard duty.

Suliven – an unusually pointy mountain in the Western Scottish Highlands.

Terp – interpreter.

Terry – Terry Taliban.

Uglies – Apache helicopters.

Zero – call sign for the command centre.

ACKNOWLEDGEMENTS

My thanks to John and Colin for their expertise
and especially to Colin for his ferocious eye for detail.

Need more Si in your life?

Get your next next Simon Ellice story from the
Rat's Tales website:
www.ratstales.co.uk

Visit the Simon Ellice Website for exclusive content,
straight from the brain of his creator.
www.simonellice.co.uk

You can also find Rat's Tales and Simon Ellice
on social media.